The Christmas Code

OTHER BOOKS AND AUDIO BOOKS

BY ED J. PINEGAR

Turn It Over to the Lord
Love One Another
Come unto Me
A Woman's Heart
I Will Follow Thee
Rejoice in Christ
On the Bright Side
Hope in Christ

THE Christmas Code

a novella by

Ed J. Pinegar

14-9-2-13-18-13-15-8-10

Covenant Communications, Inc.

Cover image: *Christmas Wreath* © Roberto A Sanchez, courtesy www.istockphoto.com

Published by Covenant Communications, Inc.
American Fork, Utah

Printed in the United States of America
First Printing: October 2014

20 19 18 17 16 15 14 10 9 8 7 6 5 4 3 2 1

ISBN 978-1-62108-848-6

Acknowledgments

I express gratitude to my sweetheart, Pat, for her listening ear. I also want to thank Emily Halverson, whose expert editing and tender heart brought magnificent ideas to the story and made it simply wonderful. To my Covenant friends Kathy and Samantha, thank you for your editorial help. And most of all, I give thanks for the inspiration from above that brought this idea to my heart.

Chapter One

Christmas carols filled the outdoor mall's expanse, echoing through the afternoon's icy December air. Frazzled shoppers darted in and out of tinseled stores, cradled in the comfort of the familiar tunes, though not necessarily aware that they were hearing them. Each with their own agenda, these consumers were preparing for the big "holiday"—which was now the only correct way to refer to Christmas. At this time of the year, it seemed so difficult to care for others because there was so much on everyone's minds and so many things to do and too few days to do it.

For some, the music playing on the loudspeakers got them in the mood to shop. But for Jeremy and his hip-hop buddies, it wasn't music at all if it wasn't rap, scratch, or beat box. With their headphones in place and pulsating hypnotic rhythms coursing from their heads to their toes, these four friends half strutted, half danced down the mall's crowded walkways, forcing shoppers to dodge out of their way.

Jeremy removed one of his earbuds to readjust it and immediately got an earful of a classic Christmas carol. Good tidings of comfort and joy? Jeremy scoffed to himself. He remembered the rent he and his friends would not be able to make that month and how the new year would probably begin with them back on the streets. Jeremy shook his head angrily. All that "comfort and joy" must have been reserved for a luckier few.

He and his buddies made their way over to the mall's central courtyard to gather at the outdoor fireplace, its cozy aroma beckoning weary shoppers to its warmth. It was there that Jeremy and his friends hung out nearly every day—that was, had hung out until some worried store owner had kicked them out for loitering or disturbing the peace. They had then headed back to their apartment complex to gather in the stairwell to make whatever trouble or fun they could. Jeremy was used to the drill and knew the world would always be against his kind. He'd learned that humanity was good at forming uninformed opinions.

* * *

Two ambitious joggers clad in the latest and most expensive running gear dashed past the mall's glowing fireplace. Chase and Alexa frequently ran this route through the outdoor mall, undeterred by freezing temperatures or the busy holiday season. Some things she could let slide, but Alexa knew full well that the ever-elusive quest for a perfect body allowed for no breaks or holidays.

She watched Chase sprint through the slushy puddles ahead and noticed she was lagging slightly behind. Not to be bested by her husband and fellow law partner at their firm, Alexa kicked her pace up a notch and felt her quads burn in reply. As she passed a children's clothing store and noticed the tiny sequined Christmas dresses gleaming in the window, she felt the familiar longing tug at her heart. Shoving the feelings aside, she ran harder.

* * *

Nearby, little Jacob was at his momma's side, pulling at her pant leg and whining for attention and treats, but like always, there were no treats to be had. Maggie Garcia was never going to be that mom. Besides, being a single parent, she had to be a mom and a dad . . . and had little money to do it with. She was convinced the population was going to hades in a hand basket with its indulgent attitude. She looked on most other parents disdainfully and refused to follow suit. In the grip of her endless to-do list, she sighed in exasperation at Jacob's pleading. "Really, son? Don't you see I don't have time for this right now?" Besides, she thought, I only need one more thing, and then I am done. Hallelujah.

* * *

An older gentleman with a tan overcoat and a tattered black scarf was looking on in amusement. He was a people watcher and often came to the mall with that hobby as his only objective. Mr. G's deeply creased face and balding hairstyle revealed his age. He had just celebrated his latest birthday alone in his cramped apartment and had even sung happy birthday to himself as his deep-set brown eyes glistened with memories of the past—seven decades filled with life's wonders, joys, and heartaches. It was the latter that often brought tears of regret rather than joy. "If only" was a phrase that haunted Mr. G's daily thoughts—thoughts he kept as private as the events that provoked them. If only I had more time to make it right, he'd say to himself as that familiar knot of worry and regret cinched his stomach tighter.

But he'd learned how to temporarily douse those flames, those ever-present reminders of his hellish past. Even the passing thought brought agony to his soul. With unrelenting drive, he quenched the flames like baking soda on a grease fire, and he trudged on through life. Most days, it was numbers, but today's remedy . . . lemon drops. Today Mr. G decided that wherever he went, whenever possible, he would share one of those old-fashioned treats with anyone he felt could use one. It was his way of soothing the wounds of the past.

Mr. G looked on as Jacob continued his begging. Like most children, Jacob was unrelenting, pushing until his mother gave up—or in this case, until someone noticed him. That frigid afternoon, Mr. G was determined to be that someone. As kindly as possible, he walked over and offered little Jacob a lemon drop. And like all little children nowadays who have been warned about strangers and candy, Jacob looked to his mother for permission. Such a sad state of affairs, our world, Mr. G thought. It was so difficult to be kind.

The mother, a lovely young woman with penetrating blue eyes, sized up Mr. G, then finally relented. "It's fine, Jacob. You can have one lemon drop."

Eyes filled with excitement, the little boy grabbed the candy and quickly popped it into his mouth.

Ever the teacher, his mom dutifully reminded him, "What do you say, Jacob?"

With a shy and hardly audible whisper, Jacob looked down and said, "Thank you."

"Good boy," the mother praised, then looked at Mr. G with a kinder expression than before and said, "Thank you, sir."

Mother and child went on their way, and Mr. G sat there in deep satisfaction—the exchange leaving all three a little less burdened. The perfect prelude for this upcoming Sunday's celebration, he thought.

A great celebration it would be, for Sunday was Christmas Day.

Chapter Two

It was Thursday morning, three days and counting until the celebration of the Christ child's birth, and the sun was peeking its head over the skyscrapers of the city. A cracked and worn door creaked open, and Mr. G slipped through it, padding down the three flights of stairs to get the morning newspaper. He wore the same threadbare slippers he'd had for years, the insoles now old rags and paper, and he sported his brand-new, secondhand bathrobe from the thrift store. It was dark blue with a golden sash that had fancy tassels on the end. It made him feel quite regal with its embroidered purple crest on the front.

As Mr. G heaved opened the heavy glass door to the building, a blast of icy air met him and cut right through his royal robe. Pulling the robe around him tighter, he scanned the cement steps below, where his paper usually sat waiting for him. It was hard to see past all the boys gathered on the steps, their cigarette smoke making a thick haze around their heads. "You're at it early this morning, gentleman," Mr. G quipped good-naturedly. And late last night as well, he added silently.

"Oh, hey, Mr. G," Jeremy said without looking up from his card game. "Yeah, gotta do our business outside so the landlady doesn't crawl all over us."

"Mrs. White doesn't mean any harm, guys. Just trying to do her business too, I reckon," Mr. G said with a gentle smile, then carefully bent over to retrieve his paper. "Hey, don't forget to check out the new sign on my door," he called out over his shoulder as he reentered the building. As far as he knew, they hadn't ever mounted the three flights of stairs to read his special messages, but he never gave up asking.

He slowly ascended the stairs himself, his breathing labored. He looked at the sign on his door again and smiled. It was an old piece of cardboard he'd thumbtacked to the wood, and it had the numbers 16-3-5-10 boldly written out in yellow, green, and gold crayon. He smiled every time he saw those numbers, in fact, for they contained a message only he understood—at least for the moment.

His landlady and neighbor across the hall, the aged and kind Mrs. White, with beautifully coiffured silver hair and soft blue eyes, had asked him what his message meant.

And he'd replied with a twinkle in his eye and a smile, which revealed a missing bottom tooth, "You keep praying, and you'll find out. You'll feel really good when you do." Then, being an old softie, he'd given hints and even the code for some of the numbers, and she'd been so tickled. She, with the help of Mr. G, was inspired by his little message.

Mr. G plopped down in his favorite overstuffed rocking chair, which formed to his body perfectly. He could eat, sleep, study, and basically do everything he cared to do in that chair, and his TV and remote were right beside it. Each morning he devoured the local newspaper, from the headlines to the comics, and he often thought as he chuckled over the comics that a good laugh was food for the soul. So laugh he did and even out loud as he ate his gourmet breakfast of skim milk and Wheaties, which he would always consider the breakfast of champions.

Then, after breakfast, he enjoyed a sudoku puzzle. Mr. G was passionate about numbers and their special meanings. He'd even created his own numerology, attaching additional meanings to each number, and had recorded these in little codebooks. He also loved colors and the special significance of each hue. It fascinated him that many of the cultures in the world found different meanings for each color. He recorded all of these findings in a notebook he'd bought from Walmart more than ten years ago; the notebook was now worn and tattered from everyday use.

After he completed his morning ritual, Mr. G rose slowly from his chair to ready himself for the day. It was Thursday—his day to walk to the park, feed the pigeons, and spread the joy of all of his secret messages with those he encountered there. After several years of carrying on this tradition, he had become quite a well-known park attraction. People began to look for him on his customary bench each Thursday, anticipating the scribbled messages he'd display on his homemade cards. He created each message from the old cardstock and crayons he'd found at the thrift store and would carefully select symbolic shades to match his coded messages.

Mr. G would encourage those who were interested in knowing more to study numerology, as well as color symbolism. Some even came to know him by name, and a few of the most ambitious would figure out the message they'd seen and return the following week to discuss its meaning and how it had affected them.

Mr. G felt these messages were one small way he could make a difference in someone's life. *Although, none of this can change my own life . . . my past. It's too late for that now*, he thought. As he slipped on his old overcoat, searing regret washed over him like a groundswell of sludge. He dropped to his knees—half moaning to himself, half praying to his God. Time was running out, and he knew it. And then it would be too late. God was so good, but . . . Mr. G had realized he had failed in so many ways.

After a few moments on his knees, Mr. G picked himself up as he always did and forced himself to move forward. There were still others he could help, if not himself. Today was special because it was the final Thursday before the great celebration.

"Sunday I will celebrate my Savior's birthday," he whispered to himself.

For many, it was simply another holiday rather than a celebration of God Almighty's Son. But today's message would change that. On a bright yellow card, Mr. G wrote out in bold red letters, "Remember to be 22-18-1-8 and 14-10-1-10-9-3-15-11, and you will make everyone around you a little happier."

After settling in on his favorite bench, Mr. G saw his two favorite parkgoers, the high-powered young lawyers Chase and Alexa, coming in his direction. Each week, they ran through the park without fail, and they had become friendly with

Mr. G to the point that the couple had started keeping track of his messages and the code used for each letter. Sometimes they would even stop to rest for a moment to discuss the message, as well as the colors Mr. G had chosen. This was the highlight of his day. Not only did someone care enough to talk to him and consider him of worth, but they also thanked him for what he had taught them and said they were blessed because of it.

"Good morning, Mr. G!" Alexa called from a distance. She and Chase slowed their pace as they crested the hill where Mr. G sat on the bench, displaying his sign.

"I'm glad to see you were undeterred by the cold this morning," Chase chirped. The couple breathed heavily from exertion, their breath creating frosty clouds in front of them.

"Why the yellow card today?" Alexa asked, intrigued. She jogged in place to keep her heart rate up, but her eyes were fastened on the coded message, and she was already trying to decipher its meaning.

In his quiet and humble way, Mr. G began softly, "Well, yellow is associated with the sun. It is the power of the earth and can produce a warming effect, radiating energy and joy to the soul. It's also cousin to white, which, in addition to happiness, also represents purity."

"And the red crayon?" Alexa prodded happily. "I'm sure there's a message there too." Mr. G could tell their encounters lifted Alexa's spirits and minimized her cares, at least for a little while.

He smiled, causing his wrinkles to gently bunch up at the sides of his eyes—eyes full of compassion and love. "You know, that red is something special. It gets your attention. It's powerful. It provokes action and promotes energy, passion, and desire. Remember to be 22-18-1-8 and 14-10-1-10-9-3-15-11, and you will make everyone around you a little happier." He gave them a little card with his message.

Chase, with deference to Mr. G, said, "Well, Mr. G, your messages always offer me and Alexa some great food for thought. Once we figure it out, I expect today's message will be no different. I guess we'll see you next week—same time, same place," Chase called over his shoulder as he continued up the hill.

"Merry Christmas, Mr. G," Alexa sang out as she took off in pursuit of her speedy partner. "See you next Thursday."

"And a Merry Christmas to you, my friends," Mr. G said quietly to himself as he watched their figures disappear over the hill. He wondered how many months he had left, sensing his Thursdays were running out. His eyes filled with tears of both gratitude and sorrow as he silently bid his friends good-bye.

Chapter Three

Others came and went as the morning wore on. Some gave Mr. G curious looks as he held his mystery message in the air, while others smiled at him knowingly and seemed to make a mental note of the code. Even the pigeons and a stray dog joined him after awhile, as they did every week.

The birds fluttered in excitement as Mr. G threw out seeds, and the dog ran and jumped around the birds, making it into quite a game. Then the mutt jumped onto the bench and put his mangy head in Mr. G's lap, and the pigeons settled down to peck at the kernels. No one ever seemed to care for the dog except Mr. G. Ted had been coming for weeks. He was a cross between a collie and a German shepherd, and he seemed to understand everything Mr. G said. Ted would sometimes nuzzle up to Mr. G and lick his hand and face, and Mr. G would smile and keep talking while Ted simply listened at the feet of his master.

As the old man shuffled out of the park later that morning, he felt a little guilty leaving Ted there all alone over the Christmas weekend. The dog must have sensed that something was different about today because for the first time, he started to follow Mr. G home. Mr. G paused for a moment, warily eyeing his loyal yet needy friend. His budget would be even more strained if he took the dog in, but he figured there could always be enough if they ate basically the same thing. With some tender, loving care, perhaps he could help Ted put on some weight and even get his coat to shine. Then he really would become a handsome dog.

These ideas trumped his financial concerns, and he slowly stooped to give Ted an encouraging nuzzle. "You want to be my new companion? My place might not be fancy, but it's warm and dry."

Ted let out an excited bark, wagging his tail furiously at the attention. "Merry Christmas to you too," Mr. G replied with a lopsided smile.

As he made his way home with his new confidant in tow, he wondered what he could give Ted in honor of this special day. If Ted was to come and go with him on his outings, he would need a collar and a leash.

Mr. G checked the mailbox and happily noted that his green-colored check was there. Uncle Sam had come through just in time! Against his better judgment, Mr. G decided he would use some of that money on Ted. He deserved it. How long had the dog been alone? Where had he come from? He was much too skinny.

No, this was going to be Ted's special day. A new home, a new collar, a new leash, and even some extra-special treats. I wonder if they make lemon drops for dogs.

* * *

Maggie spent the morning working at her part-time job at an attorney's office downtown. Thompson and Thompson was a small firm with just two attorneys, but they had a thriving and lucrative practice. The Thompsons were not only law partners but were also a married couple in their late thirties. Unable to have children, they instead focused their time and energy on building an honest and successful business.

Maggie's bosses had opted to eat lunch inside the conference room today. As she walked in to deliver the copies they'd requested, she noticed the document they were studying intently—a piece of paper with several numbers written on it.

Although Alexa was unaware of Maggie's entrance, she still spoke in hushed tones. "Kind and generous, huh? Any idea how to put this message into practice, Mr. Thompson?" she asked her husband playfully.

Maggie could see the gleam in Chase's eyes as he opened his mouth to answer and then stopped when he noticed her standing awkwardly in the doorway.

Maggie blushed cherry red and stammered, "I-I'm sorry, Mr. Thompson. I didn't mean to intrude. I just wanted to get you these documents as soon as—"

"No intrusion at all, Mrs. Garcia," Chase quickly cut her off, kindly taking the copies from her hand. "Thank you for expediting this errand. You're always right on top of things around here."

Maggie was slightly taken aback by such an open compliment. The Thompsons were never unkind to her but always seemed too mired in the cases in front of them to look up and notice anyone around them.

"Are you ready for Christmas, Maggie?" Alexa asked. She held Maggie's gaze with an expression of true interest and sincerity.

Maggie was speechless. Mr. Thompson's praise had caught her off guard enough—but extra attention from the successful and impossibly busy Alexa Thompson?

Maggie wasn't quite sure how to respond. Her words tumbled out clumsily. "Ready? Well, I don't know if a single mom could ever truly be ready. With all there is to do and buy . . . Sometimes I wonder how I'll ever pull it off. But we're making it work . . ."

So they asked you about your personal life. Fine. But did you have to make your response so personal? Her cheeks bloomed from cherry to deep pomegranate.

Chase rescued the uncomfortable moment. "Well, hopefully you're not having to work too hard. It is Christmas after all!" Maggie hadn't known he possessed such joviality. "Why don't you take the rest of the day off and take your son out for some fun? Finish whatever errands you need to get done and just enjoy yourself."

Maggie didn't know what to say, but as she started walking away, she saw Chase and Alexa smile at each other knowingly.

Chapter Four

The following day, after a delicious lunch of baloney sandwiches, Miracle Whip, and mustard, Mr. G made a simple leash out of rope for his long walk with Ted to the bank and then the pet store. Their mission? To scope out the best collar and leash for the cheapest price.

But after looking around and not seeing any in their price range, Mr. G felt sick inside. Ted needs these things. But how can I pay for his needs when I can barely meet my own?

He bowed his head and whispered a silent prayer. Minutes later, a gentle touch on his shoulder brought him back to the present. "Are you okay, sir?" the woman asked.

"Huh?" Mr. G questioned, lifting his head abruptly. A bit embarrassed, he replied, "Oh, I'm just fine, ma'am." There was something familiar about her, though he couldn't recall where he'd seen her before. But when he noticed her little boy, he instantly remembered.

The boy was one step ahead of him. "Hey, you're the grandpa who gave me lemon candy. Mommy, it's him, remember?"

As she beamed at Mr. G and nodded, he realized why he couldn't place her at first. She seemed like a completely different woman from the day before. She was smiling like the world had changed overnight.

And it had.

* * *

When Maggie and her son had returned from the mall yesterday, she'd noticed an envelope on her front door. In it had been an anonymous card wishing her family a merry Christmas, along with $1,000 in cash. Completely dumbfounded, she'd entered her house and stood there for some time as the setting sun filled the room with warmth and light. How could someone pull away from their own needs long enough to see and meet the needs of another? She couldn't decide which was the bigger miracle: that someone could be that selfless or that it had in turn created within her a selfless desire. Every penny would go toward perpetuating this miracle in someone else's life. Then it had hit her—weren't miracles what Christmas was about?

* * *

"Is this your dog?" Maggie asked Mr. G now, reaching down to give Ted's ears a good scratch. "Jacob and I love dogs. In fact, we often come to the pet store just to admire the new puppies."

"Yes, this is my new companion as of yesterday. Ted's his name. Now he just needs a proper leash and collar," Mr. G said sheepishly, and Maggie could see he was little self-conscious about the rope around Ted's scrawny neck. "Oh, and I'm hoping to buy him some dog candy. Dogs deserve candy too, don't you think?"

Maggie stood upright again, looked the two of them over, and realized her first opportunity had arrived. This humble gentleman, who had been so kind to notice and care for her son in the mall the other day, was now noticing and caring for an obviously neglected animal. He too had discovered the miracle. Maggie would not be on the outside of it any longer! She flagged down the nearest store clerk and whispered, "I need the best dog collar and leash on the market. Oh, and some dog treats too, if you have them. Lots of them."

Suddenly, Christmas wasn't just a holiday—it was a miracle day . . . and she could be a part of it.

As the store clerk went to gather the items, Maggie fidgeted nervously with her worn leather purse, then blurted out, "I know this may seem strange. We don't even know your name. But we would love to have you over on Christmas Eve . . . so Jacob could play with Ted . . . and so you could . . ." She trailed off, suddenly feeling very out of her comfort zone, unsure how her invitation would be taken.

The old man's face lit up like the star of Bethlehem. "People call me Mr. G, and I can't think of anything I'd like more! Christmases can be kind of lonely sometimes. And Ted would love it." He tried to rein in his enthusiasm, but his oversized grin gave him away.

The clerk arrived with a studded collar and leather leash. Mr. G was beside himself with joy and nervously gave Maggie a little hug. They both smiled. Maggie felt like it was right and good to hug the kind man she was helping.

Ted couldn't stop wagging his tail, and little Jacob just kept petting Ted. Maggie opened the dog treats, and Ted was in dog heaven because he had never been cared for so well or had so much attention in his whole life.

Mr. G thanked Maggie profusely for everything and especially for the invitation for Christmas Eve.

Maggie sighed, relief and joy flooding through her. "Well then, it's settled," she said. They exchanged numbers and addresses, and after she'd paid for the gifts, she gave Mr. G another hug good-bye. Then she looked down at Jacob, who had not stopped loving Ted since their conversation began, and said, "The tricky part is going to be tearing these two apart. At least it will only be until Saturday."

She looked around at the red and green decorations filling the store and felt like she was seeing it all for the first time. *So this is what they mean by the joy of Christmas.* All because an anonymous person had reached out and blessed her and her little Jacob. *Kindness begets kindness; love begets love; and we all can begin to change*, she thought.

Yet at that moment, Maggie Garcia could never have guessed the gravity of the changes soon to come.

Chapter Five

Mrs. White's floor vibrated incessantly from the bass undercurrent booming two floors beneath her. It was times like these that she wished she were a mere tenant of the building and not the landlady in charge. Jeremy and his roommates had given her ample trouble from the beginning, and she'd often wondered if the noise they created alone was grounds enough for eviction. Surely the fact that the police showed up nearly every weekend provided her a reason to let them go. But she never had the heart to follow through with any confrontation.

Yes, she was grateful that her dearly departed John had built this complex before his passing and, in so doing, had secured her future. But she often didn't feel cut out for management and would rather have been caring for others in more meaningful ways. In truth, she was lonely for companionship and craved the purpose that came from nurturing one's own family. But in this season in her life, she had neither.

And what of Jeremy's family? she wondered disdainfully. Not to mention the other boys living at that apartment. Why weren't they living with their parents? Who was caring for them, anyway? Did they not see that in the absence of an education and real work, every one of them was headed toward a dead end?

Just then, Mrs. White's phone rang. Bracing herself for another noise complaint, she was surprised to hear a request of a different nature.

"Hello, Mrs. White? It's Mrs. Davis in apartment 1-B," the voice on the other end greeted her. "Yes, my front dead bolt is stuck again, and I can't lock my door from the inside. Would you mind calling Mr. Lewis again to repair it? I really don't want to spend Christmas weekend worrying about an unlocked front door."

"Of course, Mrs. Davis. I'll contact Mr. Lewis. But you know he's not the fastest-responding handyman in the world." Mrs. White sighed. "Tell you what. I'll give him a call right after we hang up—but in the meantime, I'll just come down myself to take a look at it. I can't promise anything, but this isn't the first dead bolt that has given me trouble these past twenty years."

After leaving Mr. Lewis a voice mail, Mrs. White slipped out her front door. Mr. G's homemade cardboard sign caught her eye again as she passed his apartment door: 16-3-5-10. She remembered one of the hints Mr. G had given her. "It is what we need in order to live; it's hard to live without it." His words echoed through her mind as she thought of some of the key numbers associated with each letter.

Then it dawned on her. Of course . . . that is it! She knew the four-letter message. "Hope," she whispered.

What a delicious taste that word left on her tongue. No wonder Mr. G always seemed to have a lightness about him. What did he know and see because of this hope that she did not know and see? Although she was well aware that Mrs. Davis was waiting for her below, Mrs. White ran promptly back inside to reference her Bible, desperate to find a single verse that would further unlock this mystery. The index led her immediately to Romans 8:24. "For we are saved by hope," she whispered aloud.

Is hope the power that will ultimately save me . . . from this despair? This emptiness? But how? She read on. "But hope that is seen is not hope: for what a man seeth, why doth he yet hope for?" So what I must hope for will at first be unseen? Mrs. White closed her Bible, chewing on that thought as she descended the stairs.

As she fiddled with the dead bolt, her thoughts were far removed from her task. Though she could not put her finger on the reason, this heavenly word shined a spotlight on the pathway ahead of her. There was something in front of her now to live for; she could feel it. Hope. A familiar strain from the carol "Good Christian Men, Rejoice" floated through her mind.

Now you need not fear the grave.
Jesus Christ was born to save. . . .
Christ was born for this!
Christ was born for this!

So engrossed in this thought, she barely noticed the sound of footsteps approaching down the hallway. Jeremy's front door was just across from Mrs. Davis's, and as Jeremy turned his own key in the knob, he looked over at Mrs. White struggling with his neighbor's lock.

"Need some help with that, Mrs. White?" he offered simply.

She looked up in surprise. "Why, hello, Jeremy. If you know anything about these things, I'd be happy for you to take a look at it. I just can't see what's preventing it from turning."

But "hope that is seen is not hope."

Jeremy peered deeply into the groove where the bolt was encased. "Hmm, this might be it," he said mostly to himself as he carefully wedged the screwdriver she'd handed him into the opening. Within seconds, Jeremy had the bolt sliding in and out of the door like it was greased with freshly churned butter.

"I do declare, Jeremy. I underestimated you. Please let me pay you for this favor. What an incredible relief!" Mrs. Davis stood with her jaw agape, looking equally surprised and grateful.

"Wouldn't dream of accepting payment, Mrs. White. It was nothin'." He surprised Mrs. White when he said, "A merry Christmas to you," and slipped quietly through his doorway.

Minutes later, back in her own apartment, Mrs. White could not stop replaying the incident. Instead of judging Jeremy for his living situation, she found herself wondering with great sadness what had led him to this desperate place—and what could save him. "For we are saved by hope," she repeated aloud. "All of us."

She suddenly had an idea and marched right back downstairs to realize it with hope's bright lamp leading the way. "Christ was born for this," she sang silently. Christ was born for this.

Chapter Six

Maggie pulled into her driveway that evening with Christmas carols wafting through her car and a smile that would not leave her face. The rear door creaked loudly as she opened it to help Jacob out of the car, then they carefully made their way up the frozen sidewalk and into the house.

They had spent a wonderful Friday afternoon out and about, finishing their holiday preparations and offering Christmas cheer to anyone they could. Helping Mr. G and his dog had been the highlight for them. All Jacob could talk about the entire drive home was playing with Ted and buying him "dog candies." Maggie marveled at this infusion of joy she and Jacob were experiencing—the joy of loving and serving others—and she found herself wondering for the hundredth time who had left the money taped to her front door, jumpstarting this transformation in their lives.

* * *

After a full day out, Mr. G and Ted made the trek home with a spring of pride in their step. The brass-and-silver studded ornaments on Ted's new leather collar glinted in the setting sun. Mr. G was so pleased with the fancy collar and leash, not to mention the bag of dog candy Mrs. Garcia had found, that he nearly floated all the way home.

Spotting his apartment building in the distance, he noticed the usual gathering of Jeremy and his roommates out front. He wondered again about these boys and what had brought them together. Some of them were surely under eighteen. Why were they not in school? And where were their families?

As he got closer, however, Mr. G was surprised to find that rather than smoking and playing cards, Jeremy was hunched over the metal fencing surrounding the complex's front lawn; it had been lying on its side for some time, but Jeremy seemed to be reinforcing the base metal stakes in an effort to hoist it back up.

"It's about time that fence was up and running again," Mr. G boomed as he crossed the street. "Nice work, Jeremy."

Jeremy glanced up from his labor with a look of pride and deep satisfaction. Not unlike Ted, decked out in his new collar. Mr. G chuckled to himself.

"Hope you'll be seeing quite a few things change around here, Mr. G," he said with a smile, then turned back to the task at hand.

Something has happened since yesterday, Mr. G thought to himself with great curiosity. *Something big.*

Mr. G and Ted made their way up the three flights of stairs, and as usual, Mr. G was out of breath after the first stretch. Every once in a while, a little pain in his chest and legs and down his left arm would accompany his breathlessness. At times, even his jaw hurt. He shrugged it off as he reached the top landing just as Mrs. White opened her door.

She seemed at bit taken aback by Ted, not to mention that it was Mr. G who held the dog's leash, but an irrepressible smile spread across her face nonetheless as she greeted her neighbor. "I think I've finally figured out that mysterious sign on your door."

"That's wonderful," Mr. G responded.

"Yes, it is," she said. "And it's changed everything." After warmly holding his gaze for a long moment, Mrs. White exclaimed, "Oh, dear me. Where are my manners? Making you stand there all this time after conquering three flights of stairs! You will come in and sit for a bit, won't you?"

"I'd be delighted to, Mrs. White. Seems you've got some stories to tell," Mr. G added with merriment in his eyes.

"As do you," she said, nodding at Ted with a curious grin. "Looks like you've found yourself quite a roommate."

Mr. G beamed with pride, feeling especially grateful that Ted was outfitted in his fancy new collar for his first introduction to the landlady. "This beautiful animal here is Ted. I know some other tenants have animals, so I hope I'm not mistaken in thinking I can take him in."

"I think taking in a pet is a wonderful idea, Mr. G. Nothing sweeter in this life than the joy of good companionship. We all need to care and be cared for."

Mr. G sensed she was referring to much more than his new canine companion and nudged her further about her day. "So you said you cracked the code, did you?"

"It actually wasn't all that hard once I really set my mind to it. You see, I had a bit of a low moment this afternoon and was feeling pretty discouraged. Then I thought of you and how you always seem to manage a smile in spite of your own troubles. So when I passed by your door today, the desire to figure out your secret formula sort of overcame me. And it was just like you said: You'll—"

"Feel real good when you do," Mr. G chimed in.

"Exactly!" she said excitedly, clapping her hands. "Why, when I realized the message was hope, I ran right to my Bible to look up the first thing I could on the subject. And I learned that although hope has the power to save us, it's often something we can't see right away. Well, that got me thinking about my current situation and the hope and possibilities I have right in front of me that I just can't see right now."

Mr. G nodded encouragingly, feeling his own heart swell with hope unseen. He was remembering how he had started these messages with only the hope that they would do something for others.

"Well, then, that got me thinking about those around me in need of hope. Like that boy Jeremy downstairs. What hope does he have of a brighter tomorrow? Then the thought struck me like lightning that I could do something about that. So I marched right on downstairs and offered him a job as our resident handyman. A steady income would secure his housing here, not to mention provide him a little extra for anything he wanted to set aside for his future or what have you."

"What a marvelous idea, Mrs. White!" Mr. G praised. He couldn't help but notice how angelic his aged friend looked at that moment. With the muted afternoon sunshine spilling in from her front window, casting a heavenly glow across her countenance, he didn't think he'd ever seen her look so at peace. "That sounds like a win-win for all."

"I'll say! You know, Mr. G, I'm ashamed to say that I didn't realize how hard the poor boy has had it. After he accepted the job, he accompanied me right away to fix a leaky pipe in the boiler room. Well, we got to talking, and it turns out that boy was abandoned by his father, basically deserted by his mother, as she's been in and out of prison, and has been in more foster homes than you can shake a stick at. I've always wondered why he was out on his own so young in life. Well, 'judged him for being on his own' is probably the most accurate way of putting it. But now I see that he's never had anyone to look out for him, to help him get a fair chance at life, and I think I'm just the one to help."

"It may not be easy—you may have to spend a significant amount of your time reaching out to this boy—but I've always believed that those who can, must."

"Oh, yes, Mr. G. And you know what else I have realized? Because there will always be those who need my help, in a strange way, that means my life will always have hope and meaning. Unseen hope I can offer to help others. It's not just what my life is for but what the Christ child's was for as well. I have learned and remembered that, indeed, Christ was born for this," she said reverently as a tear streamed down her cheek. "And so was I."

Chapter Seven

Pausing on Maggie Garcia's front doorstep, Mr. G made an effort to calm his racing heart and catch his breath. Ted waited patiently at his owner's side, wagging his tail in anticipation. It took only a handful of minutes to walk to their home, but Mr. G was unusually out of breath this Christmas Eve afternoon.

In fact, he'd spent most of the morning in bed under his old calico quilt, feeling too weak to dress or even eat. He lay there for some time, fingering the loose edges of the quilt's fabric squares, staring blankly through the frosted panes of his bedroom window. As he pondered the eve of the celestial celebration before him, his heart seemed to split down the middle and pull in polar-opposite directions. He rejoiced in the holiday season yet regretted so many prior seasons of his life. There were service opportunities seized—but perhaps the most important one lost forever. There was the rescuing power of the Redeemer—but Mr. G felt that the overpowering wreckage of his past always seemed to remain.

Standing outside his hostess's house, he strained to recall the Christmas carol Mrs. White had quoted yesterday and the hope it had caused to flicker in his heart. He knew this hope was available to others—it had become his life's mission to offer it. But was it also for him?

He drew a calming breath, then gave the door a cheerful knock.

"Just a minute," a distant voice said.

Moments later, Maggie swung open the door for him and, in so doing, unleashed a nostalgic cornucopia of smells that nearly knocked Mr. G off his feet. The smells of homemade pumpkin pie, clove-scented Christmas ham, and freshly cut balsam fir brought Mr. G back to earlier Christmases in his life, to a time when places like the kitchen and the family room floor were congested with both action and joyful purpose, a time without price that was now beyond his reach.

"So nice to see you, Mr. G! Please come in and sit down," Maggie said. "You must be ready for a little rest after your walk over here." After taking Ted to the kitchen for a bowl of water, she led Mr. G into the front room and to a cozy blue-and-white gingham couch, which was situated right next to a humbly decorated Christmas tree.

"The smell of your tree fills the room, doesn't it, Mrs. Garcia? I've always favored balsam firs for that very reason. Been too long since I put one up in my own home, I reckon," he said wistfully.

"Oh, I agree. I've loved them since I was a little girl. It just doesn't feel like Christmas somehow without that aroma filling my home. Though I confess it's been awhile since I've bought one. Why, we almost went without putting up a tree at all this year—it just felt like one more expense. That is, until—" She stopped suddenly, then quietly added, "Let's just say this Christmas is turning out much different than I expected." Her eyes were aglow with gratitude and emotion.

A tiny voice filled the room with an exuberant yelp and then, "Mr. G, you're here!" Jacob ran across the room and all but jumped onto Mr. G's lap. "Did you know tomorrow's Christmas? What did you ask Santa for? Hey, where's Ted?" Like most children, Jacob fired off more questions than could be answered, then ran off to hunt for the dog. "Here boy, here boy! Where are you, buddy?"

"He's in the kitchen, sweetie," Maggie said. "In fact, let's all go in and join him. I don't know about you two, but I'm ready to dive into a good old-fashioned Christmas meal."

Maggie's spread captured everything Mr. G remembered about holiday cooking: freshly buttered homemade rolls, orange-and-clove-glazed ham, creamy scalloped potatoes. But beyond delighting his taste buds, the special meal with his newfound friends was an even bigger feast for his heart. With the three of them happily chatting away and Ted at their feet enjoying a plate piled as high as their own, it was as close to the word as he had felt in a long time. That word he never allowed himself to reflect on for long.

Family.

"Jacob, if Mr. G says it's okay, why don't you offer Ted one of those doggie candies we picked up?" Maggie then turned to Mr. G and said with a giggle, "We just couldn't help but go back and pick up some more. It's kind of like we have a dog now too."

"Oh, by all means. And you know, in a way, Ted is everyone's dog. Ever since he started visiting me there at the park—"

An unexpected knock cut off Mr. G.

Maggie jumped up to answer the door, saying under her breath, "I wonder who that could be."

"Merry Christmas!" Mr. G heard several voices say as Maggie opened her door. Then a male voice continued. "We apologize for dropping by unexpectedly. Alexa and I just had this last-minute idea of delivering Christmas goodies to a few of our hardworking employees."

Mr. G thought he recognized the voice, and hearing Alexa's name confirmed it. With great effort, he pulled himself up from his chair and slowly made his way to the door. His pace belied the excitement he felt. What were the chances that these wonderful friends somehow knew each other? "Why, it really is two of my favorite people in the world!" he boomed, trying to ignore the uncomfortable tingling down his arm. His knees suddenly went as soft as figgy pudding, and he reached out for something to steady him as the room went black.

Chapter Eight

Almost in unison, Maggie, Chase, and Alexa jumped to steady Mr. G. Chase wrapped his arm around the unsteady man. "Whoa there, Mr. G. Are you okay?"

Mr. G stiffened his legs and was able to regain his balance. He forced a chuckle. "Just got up too fast is all. Nearly fainted before I even tried to get up is the problem. I'm just shocked you all know each other! Now, how is that?" He still didn't feel quite right, but he seemed to be regaining his strength rapidly and made an effort to step away from Chase to prove he could stand on his own.

Bundled head to toe in her typical exercise attire, Alexa still looked shocked, and her jaw still hung open just shy of the frozen doorstep. "Mr. G? I had no idea you were friends with our dear secretary, Maggie Garcia! I guess this surprise has got us all feeling a little weak in the knees," she said, trying to ease the embarrassment Mr. G seemed to be feeling about the incident.

Although Maggie was equally surprised by their shared connection and deeply touched by her colleagues' visit, her worry for Mr. G overshadowed the moment. "Are you sure you're feeling okay, Mr. G? Why don't you sit back down for a bit?"

"No, no, I'll be just fine. Sitting too long was probably what did it in the first place. No, what I need right now is some fresh air and a bit of walking. But let me make sure I understand how we're all connected. You are their secretary?" he asked Maggie. "What a small world."

"Apparently it is. Yes, I've been working for the Thompsons' firm for a few months now. But how do you know these two, Mr. G?" Maggie asked.

Chase spoke up. "You know how Alexa and I cut through the park on our lunchtime runs? Well, anyone who spends any time at that park is going to know Mr. G. Every Thursday, he's there spreading his kindness to as many people as he can."

"But that still doesn't explain how the two of you are friends," Alexa said, nodding at Mr. G and Maggie.

"Let's just say it was I who was the recipient of their kindness," Mr. G said. "We actually only recently met the Garcias, but it was they who so graciously outfitted Ted here with this fancy collar and leash." He reached down to pet Ted's head, then realized he should be on his way before his strength waned again. "Are you ready to go, Ted?" he asked his companion.

Maggie stepped in closer to give him a hug. He looked her directly in the eyes and said with great tenderness, "You have made my Christmas Eve so very special. I will never forget it." Then he reached over and ruffled Jacob's hair. "Now, don't you go to bed too late, Jacob. Santa doesn't come unless you're good and asleep."

Jacob beamed with excitement. "Oh, I know, Mr. G! I'm going to bed early tonight."

They all laughed as Alexa helped Mr. G slip his coat back on. "You're sure you're not leaving on our account? We're just stopping by, you know."

"No, you can enjoy this sweet family all by yourselves. I need to get walking before the sun sinks too low. I've monopolized their time long enough," he said with a wink.

After hugging everyone good-bye, Mr. G carefully made his way down the steps and the walkway. "Merry Christmas!" he called out again, with Ted happily in tow.

* * *

Alexa watched Maggie shut the door behind her, then say, "I sure hope he does okay walking home."

"I'm sure he'll be just fine," Chase reassured her. "He's been walking to and from that park for many years. He's a tough old fella, that one. And I'm guessing he doesn't live too far from here."

"No, just a few minutes away," Maggie said, her worried look easing somewhat.

"You know, I just had an idea," Alexa said enthusiastically. "Maggie, do you happen to have Mr. G's address? What if we surprised him with a visit tomorrow, Chase? Not only would that allow us to check in on him, but we could also bring him his own plate of Christmas goodies. He's never mentioned having any family around. We may be the only visitors he gets tomorrow. Who knows?"

Maggie nodded excitedly. "What a great idea, Mrs. Thompson. I wrote down his address the other day at the pet store. I think it's in my purse in the other room. Come on in and make yourselves at home."

"We don't want to intrude for too long on Christmas Eve," Chase said. "But we'd love to get that address. That's a great idea, honey."

The two lawyers followed Maggie and Jacob into the den, where Maggie grabbed her purse and began riffling through it. Alexa studied the pictures on the wall. A black-and-white photo of a young mother sitting under a tree, with a bright-eyed toddler standing on her lap, caught her eye. Above it was a circular sign that looked like it was painted on an old pie tin. It read, "It's not enough to be Good; you must do good."

Alexa didn't know why—perhaps it was that the photograph captured the bond between a mother and a daughter—but these two wall hangings touched her deeply. "Do you mind my asking who this is in this picture?"

Still searching through her purse, Maggie took a moment to look up, then replied, "Oh, that's my saintly mother—and a very young me on her lap." She then breathed a sigh of relief as she pulled a folded piece of paper from her wallet. "Oh, good, the address."

Unexplainably curious about the photograph before her, Alexa's interrogative skills got the better of her and she questioned further. "And what about your father?" But then feeling guilty, she backpedaled a bit. "I'm sorry, Maggie. I don't mean to pry."

Maggie's face clouded over at first, but she hurriedly brushed away the emotion with a smile.

"It's fine. It's been a long time. My father left pretty early on. I actually don't remember him at all. I have some photos of my parents' wedding day," she explained, nodding at an older photo album on the bookshelf, "but that's about it."

"And what about the saying on the pie tin?" Chase prompted her, and Alexa could tell he was anxious to alleviate any discomfort either of them may have been feeling. "Is there a story behind that? It's a simple statement but a powerful one."

"It actually has double meaning. My maiden name is Good, and that saying has apparently been repeated for many generations on the Good side. My mom never changed her married name, nor did she ever stop repeating this to me. 'Remember, Margaret Good,' she'd say, 'you can't just be Good; you've got to do good too.' And, boy, did she ever live it. She was quite an incredible woman. Never remarried, raised me alone, and, as it was said of the Savior Himself, 'went about doing good' all the days of her life."

"Sounds like you've been left quite a legacy," Alexa commented quietly, almost reverently. She couldn't help but notice that this message to "do good" seemed to come up a lot in her life as of late—like a beautiful thread appearing time and again, woven by unseen hands into the very fabric of her life.

Chapter Nine

Alexa ran up ahead of Chase and gave Mr. G's door a cheerful knock. Her husband lagged behind, his arms laden with the packages and Christmas goodies they had brought.

A few seconds passed before she rapped the timeworn wood again, this time a bit harder. "I can't imagine he'd be gone already, especially this early," she said. "It's not even nine o'clock yet."

Chase tucked a large silver-and-gold package tighter under his arm and reached out with the other to give the door a hearty thump. "Merry Christmas, Mr. G," he said loudly. "It's Mr. and Mrs. Claus, and yes, we've come bearing gifts."

Suddenly, they heard clawing on the other side of the door and Ted's muffled whimpering. Chase and Alexa looked at each other simultaneously. Mr. G would not have left without his beloved new pet. Chase all but pounded on the door at this point, calling out, "Mr. G, are you in there? Open up. It's Chase and Alexa. Is everything okay?"

Overcome with worry, Alexa grabbed the door handle and started twisting and shaking it anxiously. "Is it dead bolted, or could we pick it somehow?"

An elderly woman opened her door to assess the situation, a look of concern bathing her expression. "Can I help you with something? Is everything okay?"

"I'm sorry if we disturbed you, ma'am," Chase said. "I'm sure everything is fine. I'm not sure if you know the man who lives here, Mr. G, but—"

"Why, yes, of course!" she cut him off urgently. "Not only am I his landlady, but he's also a dear friend of mine. Please tell me everything is okay. Is he home now? Was he expecting you?"

"He wasn't expecting us," Alexa explained, her brow furrowed. "But I can't imagine he'd be out this early on Christmas morning, especially without his new dog. We were actually stopping by to bring these gifts and to check on him. We were with him yesterday, and he seemed to be feeling a little under the weather."

"Oh, my," Mrs. White said somberly. "Yes, I'm with you that he would not have left Ted here alone. Oh, dear, I suppose we should try to get in just to be sure. I'll go fetch my keys."

As she left, Mrs. White realized that Jeremy still had her keys from a project he'd been working on the day before. She hated to bother him on Christmas morning, but her worry for Mr. G emboldened her. Rather than intrude in person, however, she decided to call him from her apartment.

Jeremy picked up after the first ring. "Hello?"

"Hello, Jeremy. It's Mrs. White. I hate to bother you on Christmas, but I'm afraid I need you to bring me up my keys. And in a hurry."

Within minutes, all four of them were in front of Mr. G's door, holding their breath as Jeremy inserted the master key. As he slowly cracked the door open, everyone was taken by surprise as Ted bounded out and started to excitedly jump on each one of them.

"Whoa, boy. It's okay, Ted," Chase said as he crouched down to give the dog an encouraging pat. "We love you too, buddy."

"Mr. G?" Alexa called out uncertainly, now a bit self-conscious that they were inside his home without permission. "Mr. G, it's Alexa Thompson. Are you in here?"

"The bedroom is back that way," Mrs. White offered, gesturing toward the right. "Go on back there while the rest of us wait here. He's probably still sleeping, that's all."

Alexa followed the hallway to Mr. G's bedroom. Midmorning sunlight streamed through the sheer window coverings. She saw his large, motionless form under a homemade calico quilt and inhaled sharply. "Mr. G?" she whispered.

Ted ran around her, then put his paws up on Mr. G's bed by the pillow, licking his master's face. Alexa came closer and saw that although Mr. G's eyes were closed, his face was wet with tears. It appeared as though Ted had not been trying to rouse his new owner but to comfort him.

"Mr. G, are you awake?" Alexa said a bit louder, covering his leathery hand with her own.

His eyelids fluttered, and he reached up weakly to wipe away the moisture and fatigue.

"Mr. G. It's Alexa. Are you okay?"

"I . . . I . . . I think so. I was in terrible pain. I tried to get up . . . All I could do was lie here and think about . . . about them. I never got to apologize or explain . . ." His face darkened, the tears flowing freely again.

Chase called from the other room. "How is he, Alexa? Is he awake?"

"He's okay," she called back. "Just very weak. You can come back."

Chase, Mrs. White, and Jeremy approached the doorway together with concern clouding their expressions.

"He's okay now, but he says he did have a lot of pain earlier," Alexa told them.

"Oh, man, Mr. G, you got my heart pumpin' this morning, racing up those three flights of stairs. Guess you finally found a way to get me up here." Jeremy made an effort to speak lightheartedly, but the worry in his eyes gave him away.

"I think we should call the doctor," Mrs. White said decidedly. "Of course, the holiday might make this tricky."

"No, no," Mr. G protested feebly, lifting his wrinkled hand off the quilt. "Don't bother my doctor today. Everything is fine and as it should be."

He looked so vulnerable lying there, his face so pale and damp that Alexa didn't have the heart to overpower his fragile wishes.

Mrs. White felt the same way. "Well then, I'll leave you in the care of your friends here," Mrs. White said, then turned to the Thompsons and continued. "Please let me know if you need anything. I live right across the hall in apartment 3-A. I'll be sure to check on him later after you leave."

Mrs. White and Jeremy quietly excused themselves, but Mr. G hardly seemed to notice.

He was still crying. "Please do not worry about me, my friends. The pain I feel right now is not physical. You see, when you reach the end of your life, you can't help but think about all you did wrong and what you might have done differently. I'm afraid for me, it's too late." He spoke in barely audible tones.

Chase and Alexa sensed that what their friend needed right then was not words but a listening ear. They came a little closer and sat at the foot of his bed.

"Go on," Chase encouraged gently. "What's troubling you, Mr. G? You will find no judgment here."

It was as if that merciful statement alone broke a dam in his heart, and the waters that trickled therefrom suddenly turned into a rushing torrent of pain. Mr. G sobbed openly, barely able to get out the words. "It's been nearly forty years since I lost my wife and child. Not a day has passed that I haven't hated myself for that." He turned his head toward the wall and spoke with his eyes closed, confessing to no one and anyone who would hear him, including God. "Early on in our marriage, not long after our first child, I became depressed and started to drink. And like so many who get hooked on alcohol, I found my life heading downhill in a hurry. It affected us all. I lost my job teaching at the middle school, and not long after that, my marriage really began to fall apart. Then, finally, when my wife could no longer handle the pressure and trials of an alcoholic husband, she left a note that said, 'Dear Matthew,'" Mr. G coughed, then choked out the rest of the words of the letter. "'I can't stand it any longer. I'm sorry for you. You were once a good man but now . . . Mary.'

"A few days later, after finally sobering up, I realized what had happened. I searched and searched to no avail. Neither Mary nor I had any siblings, and both sets of parents were gone. None of her friends knew where she went either. She just vanished."

He paused for a moment to compose himself. Alexa held on to his hand tightly, her own face streaming with tears. She saw Chase swallow hard with emotion at the sight of this near-perfect man who was still in the grips of his imperfect past, never feeling that he was worthy or deserving of the goodness and tender mercies of God he knew filled the lives of others.

After several moments, Mr. G went on. "I never stopped searching. I put ads in the paper, their pictures on telephone posts. I never did involve the police or press charges of any kind as far as my daughter was concerned. I knew why Mary had chosen to leave and figured that as an adult, she had the right to do so. After all, she was only protecting herself and her daughter . . . our daughter," he corrected, his voice thick with emotion. "More than anything, I wanted to find them so I could apologize. Words will never repair what I've done, but I have longed to say them anyway, to express the guilt and sorrow I've lived with every day of my life. I've yearned for them to know, in spite of my weakness, how truly loved they were . . . and are." Mr. G's face twisted with pain at the thought of lost opportunities and a wasted life.

He pulled out a small framed picture from under the covers and turned it toward the couple. "That's my wife Mary and our little Margaret when she was not even two."

Alexa looked into the eyes of the woman in that black-and-white photograph and felt as though lightning had shot through her. "Mr. G, this may seem odd to ask right now, but what is your last name?" she asked.

"Never felt worthy of it, which is why I don't go by it. But for better or worse, my last name is Good."

Electricity pulsed through Alexa once again. Unable to hold herself back, Alexa jumped up and blurted out, “Chase, you stay right here with Mr. G, and I’ll be right back. And Mr. G, will you trade that photograph for this homemade fruitcake I baked for you? I just now realized there’s something else we should have brought.” Alexa was out the door at a full sprint before anyone could respond.

Chapter Ten

Shoving aside the fancy department-store bags and boxes filling her backseat, Alexa made room to throw in her winter coat and purse before jumping behind the wheel. These symbols of Christmas consumerism seemed so empty and meaningless to her now. Now, swallowed up in realities such as family and forgiveness, life and death, Alexa didn't know whether to weep or sing out with joy. Instead, she pressed the gas pedal to the floor and raced to the Garcias' with all the fury of wild horses, praying she wouldn't be too late.

She hesitated for only a moment on the doorstep. Was she certain enough about Maggie's possible identity to make such a life-altering claim? She glanced down again at the worn picture frame trembling in her hands. The love in that mother's face, that connection between parent and child, there was no mistaking it. She knocked loud and quick.

Maggie opened the door almost immediately, anxiety etched deep in her face. "Mrs. Thompson? I'm surprised to see you. Is everything all right?"

"Mrs. Garcia . . . Maggie . . . please forgive me for intruding on your Christmas festivities, but there is something I think you should see," Alexa said hurriedly.

"Something I should see?" Maggie echoed slowly, bewilderment filling her eyes.

"Yes, you and Jacob need to come with me right now. You are not going to—" Alexa stopped herself midsentence, realizing how crazy she was about to sound, so she instead thrust the worn frame into Maggie's hands. "Look," she instructed, "and tell me if the people in this photo look familiar to you."

Maggie studied the photo, her posture frozen, her face growing paler with each passing moment. "How did you—" she whispered in a tone barely audible, then demanded more loudly, "Alexa, where did you get this photograph?"

Without waiting for a response, Maggie spun on her heels and ran into the back office. Alexa followed her and watched as she yanked the old photo album she had shown Chase and Alexa just the night before off the shelf, throwing it open and turning swiftly to a page she seemed to have memorized.

Maggie and Alexa both gasped as the exact same picture in the frame appeared on the yellowing album page before them.

"Maggie, please. There is no time to stand here and explain. You must go get Jacob and come with me. Now!"

The tearful daughter needed no further proof. Not seconds later, with little Jacob at her side, Maggie ran out the door toward a moment Alexa was sure she had dreamed of her entire life.

* * *

As the three of them slipped into the apartment without a knock, the silence that met them was deafening.

Alexa led the way into the back room, worry etched on her face at the sight of her husband slumped over with his head in his hands. Maggie saw Mr. G's body lying peacefully yet motionless on the bed, and her heart plummeted.

"He hasn't spoken since you left, Alexa. And his breathing continues to slow," Chase whispered almost to himself. Then he looked up to meet his secretary's gaze. "Dear Maggie, I'm so sorry. Come closer, please. Take my seat right here."

Maggie sat on the edge of the bed as close to the still form as she could get and let out a quiet sob. "Dad? Daddy, it's me . . . your little Margaret. Please don't go. Alexa told me everything. Oh, Daddy, I forgive you."

Through tears, she looked at the pained yet glowing countenance of this magnificent man—a man she had grown to love before really knowing who he was. A man who had reached out to notice and love her son before even knowing he had deeper reasons to. In some celestially orchestrated way, their lives had intersected to allow them to love and be loved without titles or introductions. Maggie had no doubt that before her was a pure and purified soul, for he had offered his love to them before even knowing that he knew he should.

Mr. G's eyelids suddenly lifted, almost imperceptibly. "Margaret," he whispered weakly. "Margaret, is it really you?" He strained to focus his eyes. "Maggie?" he said as he looked at her in both confusion and recognition.

"Yes, Daddy, it's me. It is God who has brought us together again. I wish Mom could be here too."

"Oh, Margaret, I just had the most wonderful dream," he said softly, looking at her with all the tender love a father could give. "Margaret, God has forgiven me. This now I know. And your mother came too. She came to me and told me it was time. I guess more Good is needed on the other side," he somehow managed to quip with a twinkle in his eye.

Maggie knew the goodness of God had entered her father's soul. His guilt had been swept away. He was free. He was clean. He was happy as he prepared to return to his heavenly home with his cherished Mary.

He and Maggie held each other's hands tightly and looked deeply into each other's eyes, and Jacob and Ted looked on from the foot of the bed.

Then peacefully, Mr. G's eyes slowly closed for the last time. He had overcome.

The room was silent and yet charged with a heavenly energy that lasted for quite some time. No one dared move, fearing to disturb the holiness that lingered. Through her tears, Maggie noticed an open notebook next to her father's head on the nightstand. She felt compelled to reach for it and began to read aloud the last page it was opened to . . . "Gratitude for the Goodness of God."

As Maggie mused over her dad's last words, Ted let out a joyful bark and wagged his tail in what appeared to be admiration for his master.

"Ted," Maggie said, brushing away the tears, "you will come live with Jacob and me now. Somehow, I think that too was meant to be." She softly closed the notebook and drew both Jacob and the dog close.

From across the room, Chase gestured toward the book, then stepped closer. "I just noticed the numbers on the front of that journal. May I?" he asked gently.

"Of course," she said softly.

Alexa joined her husband as he read the cover aloud.

14-9-2-13-18-13-15-8-10
For the Goodness of God

"Of course that would be the title," Alexa voiced with deep emotion. "Gratitude. Gratitude for the Goodness of God."

* * *

Several days later, these four friends, along with Jeremy, Mrs. White, and only a few others, stood side by side at Mr. G's graveside. A temporary monument had been placed at its head until the final stone was completed. It read simply:

Matthew Good
A man who showed with his life
That it is not enough to be Good
But to do Good—
And thus he did.

Alexa and Chase walked home from the cemetery, cutting through the park where they had first met Mr. G only a few months ago. Alexa thought about where she had once been and, because of this good man, where she was now. The emptiness in her heart gave way to excitement as she linked her arm through Chase's and drew him close. "I'm pregnant, sweetheart."

Chase pulled away slightly to look at her in disbelief. When he met no humor but only honesty in her gaze, he shouted for joy and lifted her off her feet.

"And if it's a boy," she added, "we'll name him Matthew."

Mr. G's Code

2	4	6	8	10	12	14	16	18	20	22	24	26
A	B	C	D	E	F	G	H	I	J	K	L	M

1	3	5	7	9	11	13	15	17	19	21	23	25
N	0	P	Q	R	S	T	U	V	W	X	Y	Z

Mr. G's Color Code

Red—energy, passion, life, vitality, confidence, enthusiasm, courage, and action.
Pink—peace, love, soothing, nurturing, tenderness, acceptance, beauty, relaxation, and calm.
Yellow—joy, wisdom, love, happiness, optimism, cheerfulness, and uplifting.
Green—nature, fertility, life, restfulness, balance, growth, rebirth, harmony, and balance.
Blue—spirituality, soothing, truth, trust, serenity, calm, peacefulness, and youth.
Gold—wisdom, prosperity, divinity, power, and preservation.
Silver—energy, emotion, sensitivity, respect, courteousness, compassion, and justice.
Purple—royalty, dignity, creativity, good judgment, imagination, and spiritual fulfillment.
Black—the absence of color.
Brown—serious, earthy, security, protection, and warmth.

White—purity, cleanliness, new beginnings, equality, divinity, innocence, fairness, wholeness, perfection, and completeness.

When you see these colors, let your mind be positive and act in righteousness.

About the Author

Ed J. Pinegar is the author of over fifty nonfiction and audio products. He has been a lifetime teacher of the youth. He is passionate about the life and teachings of Jesus Christ, who gives hope to all, and it is Ed's Christmas wish that all may have hope and come to realize with gratitude the goodness of God. He and his wife, Pat, are the parents of eight children, thirty-eight grandchildren, and eighteen great-grandchildren.